Lost in Wildcat Cove

The Critters of Wildcat Cove #1

By Dr. Sandra Cook

With Illustrations by Laura Merris
Edited by Ryan P Freeman

This book is dedicated
to all children who have ever needed
a friend.

It was a bright and sunny day in Wildcat Cove and the days were becoming warm with the arrival of spring. In the trunk of an old tree a mother chipmunk awaited the arrival of her newborn babies. The mother chipmunk guarded her burrow so that her babies would be safe when they arrived. As the sun set one spring evening her babies were born. The first one was born, then the second, the third, and finally the fourth.

The mother chipmunk named her babies Charley, Chelsey, Chula and the fourth, the smallest little chipmunk, Chippy. Mother chipmunk watched over her babies day and night. She took good care of them as they grew bigger and bigger. The babies were brown with white stripes and little white spots on their backs. They were very tiny just like a small mouse.

As the babies grew, Charley, Chelsey, and Chula began to explore their burrow. They began to peek cautiously out of the burrow at the world around them. But the bravest little chipmunk was Chippy. He watchfully stepped out of the burrow and began to explore.

Chippy saw that there were many trees all around him. There were big trees and small trees, each one beginning to show signs of spring as their leaves were beginning to grow buds on their branches. The ground under his little feet felt soft, cool, and wet from the spring rains.

As he continued to explore, the ground beneath his feet began to get wet and squishy. Soon he came upon a sight that he did not understand. Something was splashing and sprinkling him. His fur began to feel different than it had ever felt before. Chippy shook his fur and as he did he saw what was sprinkling on him. There in front of him was a very large hole in the ground with something wet. *"How curious,"* Chippy thought. *"I wonder what this is,"* Chippy queried.

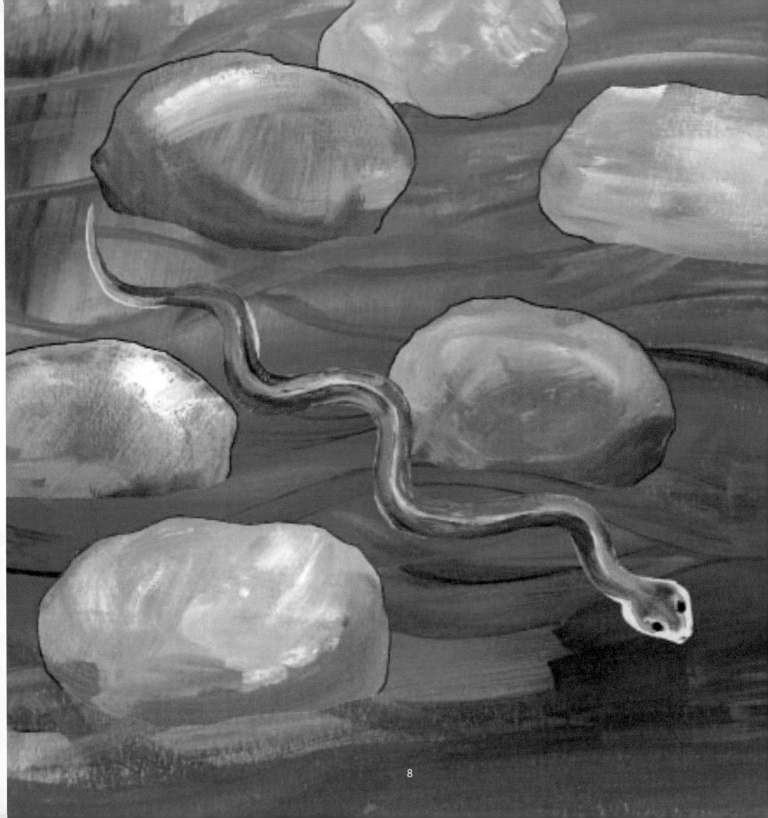

As Chippy pondered his thoughts he heard the splashing of waves hitting the shore; he moved closer to the sound and found himself face to face with Simon.

"Who are you?" Chippy asked.

"My name is Simon, what is yours?"

Chippy happily answered, "My name is Chippy, I am a chipmunk. You don't look like a chipmunk."

Simon hissed back, "that is because I am a sssssnake. I live here in the water along the shore of the lake. Where do you live?"

Chippy couldn't understand why but he began to get a little wary of Simon, he answered gingerly, "I live in that big, old tree up the bank with my mother, brother and two sisters."

Simon perked up at the thought of the chipmunk family living so close to shore. Simon began to smile his mischievous smile and hissed at Chippy saying, "Why don't you bring your brother and sisters here to play? There are lots of rocks to hop on and tree limbs to jump from one to another."

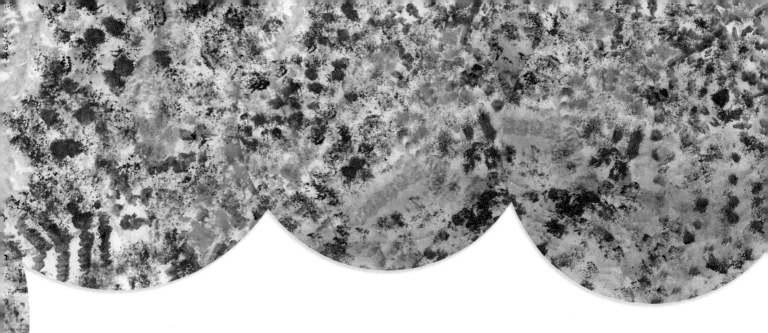

But Chippy began to grow more wary of Simon now. He did not know why he was so nervous but he decided he needed to continue on his journey. As he moved closer to the other trees to see if anyone lived there, he began to notice that he did not know where he was or how to get home. Chippy was lost. How was he going to get home? He was certain that his mother would be very worried about him. Chippy began to get really scared. He must find a way to get home.

As he looked around to find that big old tree, he came upon Greta Groundhog. Greta Groundhog sat in the shrubs and squeaked "Hello" to Chippy as he came near.

"Hello," Chippy chirped.

Now Chippy looked at Greta and thought that she kind of looked like him. Her tail looked like his and her fur was brown like his, but she was bigger than he was and her ears were tinier than his. Chippy noticed that she didn't have the same stripes or spots on her body like he did. Still he felt that maybe she could help him find his mother and brother and sisters.

"Can you help me find my family?" Chippy asked.
Greta Groundhog was a very nice groundhog, she wanted to help but she was busy gathering food for her own babies. How could she get food back to her hungry babies if she stopped to help Chippy get home? So Greta asked, "Where do you live?"

Chippy answered, "We live in the big, old tree up the bank."

"Well then," Greta Groundhog replied, "I will help get you as far as I can while I gather food for my babies."

Chippy was thrilled and offered to help Greta gather food on their way back to the big old tree up the bank.

As they journeyed through the cove toward the big, old tree up the bank, Chippy told Greta about meeting Simon. Greta's eyes opened wide and she gasped and said, "Oh my dear, do not listen to Simon. He is tricky and not very nice to the other animals."

Chippy didn't understand. Simon just wanted to play, didn't he? Yet something about Simon did make Chippy wary.

Chippy and Greta continued on their way through Wildcat Cove gathering nuts, conifer cones, and plants for Greta's babies when they soon came to a little creek. Resting beside the creek on the cool, muddy edge was a turtle.

The turtle peered from his shell and studied the couple in front of him, "Who are you?" he asked.

"We are Chippy Chipmunk and Greta Groundhog, what is your name?"

"Timmy Turtle is my name and racing is my game."

Now Chippy was new to Wildcat Cove so he had a lot to learn, but Timmy did not look like a racer to him. Timmy had short stubby legs that could barely get him up off the ground and he carried a hard, brown shell on his back. The shell looked heavy and seemed to keep Timmy's feet far apart.

Chippy asked, "How can you race with that shell on your back, Timmy?" Timmy smiled his slow and sincere smile and answered, "I can race because I do not give up. I keep going no matter what gets in my way."

Now Chippy started to get discouraged and scared about finding his mother. Timmy sounded like a very smart turtle. *Maybe Timmy can help*, he thought to himself.

"Timmy do you think you can help me find my burrow and my mother?"

Timmy pondered that request and replied, "Chippy, although I am a racer I am slow on my feet, but I will help you find the courage to continue on with your search."

So, as the three new friends continued on they helped gather food for Greta Groundhog's babies and were ready to meet any challenge that came their way.

The friends continued on their journey, when they came to a log laying in the cove blocking their path. Now for Chippy and Greta this was no problem, but how was Timmy going to get to the other side? He couldn't jump like Chippy, or climb like Greta, he could only crawl with that big heavy shell on his back. As the three friends sat pondering their problem, who do you think came slithering out of the log? Simon the snake came hissing up to them.

"Well hello my friends." Simon mocked. "Who are your friends Chippy? Have you come to play with me?"

Chippy remembered what Greta Groundhog said about Simon Snake being tricky and not being very nice to the other animals. So Chippy replied shyly, "No, we are heading up the bank and need to help Timmy Turtle get past this log."

Simon Snake grinned with a dangerous smile and meanly said, "You won't be able to get him over that log. His legs are too short and he has that heavy shell on his back. Just leave him and come play with me."

Chippy looked at Greta questioningly. Greta moved toward Chippy and gave him a little nudge and said, "Come on Chippy, let's help Timmy find a way to get to the other side of the log and find your mother".

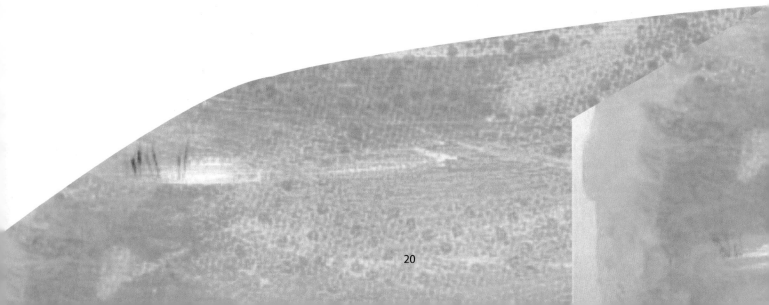

As Chippy and Greta began to think of how to help Timmy get past the log, Simon started to make fun of Timmy. "He hides in his shell, and moves so slow," teased Simon.

Chippy did not think that Simon was being very nice to Timmy. So the brave little chipmunk went up to Simon and said, "You are not being very nice. Timmy is a friend of ours and we like him just the way he is."

The three friends continued to try and solve their problem with the log that was blocking their way. They looked around and saw another log leaning against the log that was blocking their path. They decided to see if Timmy could walk up the log to get across to the other side so they could continue on their way.

Chippy and Greta helped Timmy climb up the log and make it over their obstacle. Once Timmy made it over the log the friends continued on gathering food for Greta's babies and looking for the old tree up the bank.

Finally the three friends walked up the bank and spotted the old tree up the bank where Chippy lived with his mother and brother and sisters. Chippy was excited to be home and to see his mother and his mother was very happy to see him. She had been very worried about her brave little chipmunk.

Chippy enjoyed his adventure in the cove and making new friends along the way. He learned how important it is to be a friend and to never give up.

Made in the USA
Monee, IL
27 December 2020